Garden Variety

Garden Variety
An anthology of flower poems

Lily Contento
Editor

QUATTRO BOOKS

Editor: Lily Contento
Contributing Editors: Allan Briesmaster, Luciano Iacobelli, Beatriz Hausner
Cover Design and Typography: Julie McNeill, McNeill Design Arts
Cover Artwork: Veronica Brownstone
Photo on back cover: Tierre Taylor

Library and Archives Canada Cataloguing in Publication

Garden variety : an anthology of flower poems / Lily Contento, editor.

ISBN 978-0-9782806-4-2

1. Canadian poetry (English)–Ontario–Toronto Region.
2. Canadian poetry (English)–21st century.
3. Flowers–Poetry. I. Contento, Lily

PS8295.7.T67G37 2007   C811'.6080364   C2007-906003-X

Published by
Quattro Books
P.O. Box 53031
Royal Orchard Postal Station
10 Royal Orchard Blvd.
Thornhill, ON L3T 3C0

www.quattrobooks.ca

Contents

Preface

The earliest recollection I have of playing with flowers goes back to grade five, and it all happened on a balcony. That year, during a biology lesson, I learned something about crossing plants to alter their appearance. I can't remember the details of the lesson, but I can remember feeling that it would be magic if I could cross a white flower with a red one and eventually get a pink bloom. So immediately after school one day, I went home, grabbed a pair of scissors, a roll of string and proceeded to cut off the stems of the massive geraniums my mother had been growing on her balcony for years. Then, I performed a diagonal slit on the remaining plant stubs, attached them to the previously severed geraniums, and finally tied each one with string.

I couldn't wait to see what would bloom. But more than that, I anticipated with elation my mother's happiness at the sight of the new hybrids of geraniums that would grow on her balcony. They would be the best geraniums in Naples, perhaps even in all of Italy. If I was lucky enough, I would get a multitude of colours in one flower. Wow.

But that was that. Nothing grew. My mother on the other hand was furious (to put it less loud than it was) and I believe that was when she began to think there was something seriously strange with her child.

I have been trying to make peace with flowers ever since. First through the various gardens in my life: uprooting old plants, transplanting them to new spots for just the right amount of sun, reading books to understand the subtleties of garden design. But to be frank, I have yet to create the perfect garden or anything close to it – most likely I never will. My quest to give birth to an oasis of flowers, a garden that will speak of luscious dreams, continues.

Then, a few years ago, after leaving the education world, I retrained as a florist and eventually opened my own shop, which I love. Next to writing, working with flowers is all about life. Even if working with flowers is tough work, and my hands often swell rough, I love the smell, the colours, the textures that surround me. I live in beauty all day long.

Lately I've been writing poetry about flowers. This is how this book began: flower after flower, poem after poem, I was tempted by the idea of a collection of flower poems. The thought was provoking. What if writers in the community wrote the poems? The idea grew. An anthology of flower poems – why not. After all does not *anthologia* – from the New Latin, and earlier, from the Greek – mean "flower gathering"?

Before I knew it, with the help of poets, editors and graphic designers, we had begun to enthusiastically turn-up the soil. We had begun to make imaginary flower beds for writers to sow their imagination in. Eventually, we realized we had a familiar yet enticing literary garden.

More than 80 poets submitted poems, all of which were simply captivating, so much so that it became a painful task to choose which would be published and which would not. As it is true with planting flowers, as we chose the poems for the anthology, we had to forgo beautiful ones to achieve the overall effect of the garden anthology. What we finally had in our hands was a collection of flower poems, which essentially grew into an inviting, sensuous albeit sometimes prickly garden.

Garden Variety is ground fertile with brilliant poems, which sometimes modestly, sometimes violently, often provokingly, speak of flowers. The poems have been arranged as if they were real flowers in a garden, collected into flower beds, not exactly how they would look in an everyday garden, but more like they appeared in our minds when we were choosing them for publication. We considered height, colour and season when we organized our poetry garden, and hope you will sense their beauty as much as we did.

This literary garden is a communal garden in the streets of Toronto. It belongs to everyone. It belongs to us.

I invite you to enter our Garden, taste the sweetness of the lilies, believe the rose opens flesh alive, watch the blue delphinium rise breath after breath. Walk around this garden and know you are among friends.

Let yourself go.

Lily Contento

Ewan Whyte

Fioretti (of St. Francis)

Alone in silence
after a wealthy party

Resting for shelter
in a half fallen country chapel

Looking out over the fields
through the holes in the walls

He took off his rich clothes

For a week he spoke with sister moon
and brother sun

hearing their songs in inflected light

After the last night at the first
moments of dawn

when the sun sends its sheets of fire
over the living surface of the earth

He woke with joy and shuddered
to the opening of the fields of flowers.

Steven Michael Berzensky

Lotus One

in
no
                        peril
        from
this
                muck
not
                stuck
in
it
        floats
this
        flowering
                        pearl

Paul Dutton

BLUEBELL

pe(t)al

Rob Rolfe

Nasturtiums

in the garden
nasturtiums
dying cucumbers
wounded lettuce
the coriander
has not survived
the peppers
the sweet basil
the oregano
all have come
to maturity
in the heat
but the garden
is slowly
dying the red
is more fiery
on its last legs
I am pleased
you painted
the nasturtiums
they waited
so long to flower
to perfect
this intensity
soon to die

Ronna Bloom

The Good Plant

You sent me a plant
and it died. Not right away
but soon after.
Every year you send me the same plant
and every year, it dies. I dread
its arrival: its lovely pink heads
bobbing down the hall on the arms
of the large delivery man.
Every year at this time the plant comes
with a card: a sweet new year, a healthy year,
a happy, healthy year. And every year it dies.
Was I doing something wrong,
placing it too close to the light, not close
enough? This year I read the instructions carefully,
the ones that come stuck in the earth.
They said: a hand passed between flower and window
should cast a definite shadow. And mine did.
They said: keep the earth slightly damp. And I did.
They said: ornamental plant, do not eat. And I didn't.
Still, today its bright pink heads fell
and I got so mad I wanted to pluck them off:
dead again, I thought and watered them for no reason.
The heads came back a little, roused themselves.
But I don't trust this revival.
The truth is
they don't want to be here,
you just send them.

16

Gale Zoë Garnett

Baby's Breath

Children see mythically

But

Are not metaphorical

The lady said

The little white flowers

Were baby's breath.

I put my ear to the bouquet

There was no sound

No sound at all.

The babies are dead

I told her

Lynn McClory

Rescue Remedy

She drops flower essence under
her tongue 3x's a day since it happened

Clematis for dreaming the future without a plan
Rock Rose for terror in the night
Star of Bethlehem against its shock
Impatiens for impatience
Cherry Plum for fear of her mind giving way

Any wilted flower that imbibed this
tincture will concur
as it stands in the present drenched in awe
waiting for the sun to ignite its fire and
the remedy to release this honeysuckle longing

Sue Sinclair

Roses

Not because it is sufficient, but because
we subsist on light, and what doesn't
cry out to be noticed? There's something here
you might recognize, but you're not sure; still, you're willing
to risk it: the loss is of everything, seen and unseen,
the before and the after. It doesn't depend on you
but you move toward it. Because as long as there's a moment
here or there, why not arrange a few roses
in a jar, give thought to their listlessness, how they gather
the room about them yet think nothing of it, how each
thorn persists, how they have made a purpose
of holding still? Then you remember
the necessary and sufficient. This isn't it,
but you don't know where else to begin.

Paul Zemokhol

Posy

The world is more backwards
than I know

it calls back the ratchet
of things
Ipswitches the handsprings
calumnies the Calumets
all in the name of
Philodendron.

others are redoubted,
crossed to their
suffering,
fulminate of Barbary,
all those tinges
which make the honest
ones cringe.
even hibiscuses blush, flush
with shame.

The world is more backwards
than I know

rewrite the recombined,
Castigliori castigated,
conundrums beaten
humdrum
to a paint colour
that pleases mums.

The world is more backwards
than I know

orange is how to look
below the above
and abutting
the beagle's musings.
Corrugate the correct;
its erect corrosions
fall the footsteps
to hollows where
lilacs loll.

The world is more backwards
than I know

a few more lines
before the ink dries
with the cries of myself
in tow.
I ask the lies,
at trials of spies,
a rose's red
eyes.

The world is more backwards
than I know.

Gary Michael Dault

The Orchid in Very Early Air

At four o'clock in the morning
before the birds begin to sing
and the room is solid with cold

the orchid is seized
with temptation:
the air offers it
the perpetual blueness
of non-breathing

but the orchid will not
flame out,
growing redder and redder
instead
like a struck match

until the whole house
is warm to the touch

Jaclyn Piudik

Recipe To Overcome Loneliness While Waiting for a Lover...

1.
Take the residue of his kiss,
chew it well and spit
into a bottle of old ewe's milk.
Boil these contents
in an overturned vat.

A skin will form.
Remove it ever so gently and wear it
as if you were the sea in two dimensions.
Coat yourself
and you will tingle as if he were near you.

(Remember, the illusion of realness is precious.)

2.
In the hot liquid, steep
29 savage blossoms
patiently cultivated from the field
just north of your love.
Sniff. The vapor will be his.
Taste. As it mingles it becomes yours.

Add an ounce of twisted bark,
cover with burlap
and a preferred piece of lace.
Then wait.

3.
Let stand...
Until you cross into the numbness of being seen,
stop fighting the ravaged days of an obligatory present,
resurrect the dream in unbroken shades of green.

He is tall and doesn't play the lute.
You travel between mud and silk.

4.
When you wake out in the open grove,
exfoliate virtuous layers.
Enter into the eighth age of your life,
into a newly pruned rose garden
where there is room for thought.

West of your want your balm is thickening.

Kildare Dobbs

A Prayer at Parting

Let music carry you, with flowers
that blossom for you in all the parks
and green gardens of the great city,
wallflowers, peonies and roses
in airs blended with your gentle breath
that lapsed with a sigh just before dawn
since when all we have is your absence
which lingers like the scent of sweetpeas
or the echoes of lost happiness.

Robert Priest

The Uncatchable Man

There was once an uncatchable man and nothing could catch this man, not traps, not houses, not colds, not people with nets, nothing could catch him because he was free and easy and he couldn't be nailed down. He just travelled around in search of a special jewel he was after and would slip out of any sticky situation with a high squeal and some very fine rolling. Eventually, the uncatchable man found his way to a certain pollen patch and, being very white, he decided to roll there, taking on for a while the fabulous rainbow hues of nature. While he was rolling there, rolling and laughing about how easily he had always evaded capture, the resident butterfly came by and asked him, "How are you liking the trap?" "What do you mean the trap?" he asked. "The trap you're in," the butterfly replied. "You are caught in a butterfly trap." "Ah-ha-ha!" the man laughed, for he knew the butterfly was wrong and that nothing could catch him. "Well, why don't you leave then?" the butterfly asked. "I could leave if I wanted to," the man yelled, continuing to roll – rolling, if anything, more joyfully and laughing louder and louder as he moved deeper and deeper into the pollen trap, rolling and laughing and thinking about how much capture he had evaded and chortling with shrill glee. "Bet you can't get away now," the butterfly screamed above him. "Bet you like the trap now!" "O how I love the trap!" the man yelled. "I love the trap – so much fun to get away from. So much fun to roll like this, right up to the stickiest flowers themselves and then run away." Saying this the man pointed to the bent-down lips of a huge pollen-swollen flower which was at the very heart of the trap. "Aaaaah, what a sweet flower!" he said in a high hysterical voice, observing with great appetite the sticky climb of pollen higher-up the blue and red and purple petals. Suddenly he felt a great urge to stick his face right up one of the large floral bells. "Watch this," he said to the butterfly, and getting down on his multi-coloured knees and folding back his pollen-smeared wings he ducked his head down under, right up into the open mouth of it. "O sweet, sweet sticky colours!" the man giggled from within, letting the multi-coloured syrups ooze down onto his shoulders and draw him in. "O sweet and tasty flower!" he bellowed. And then of course, just as it looked like he had been captured, he popped out with a shriek of triumph, jumping up and down mockingly in front of the butterfly. "Well, bye-bye butterfly," he said, turning his back on her as he ran across the pollen patch and out into the world. Bitterly the butterfly watched the uncatchable man go running, and then she returned weeping to her nest at the top of the flowers. Some day her tender blossoms would be restored. Some day she would catch a mate. Sadly, sadly as the moonlight fell and the great whoops and shrieks of laughter of the uncatchable man faded into the starlight and dew, the tears of the butterfly dripped down the stalks of her flowers and formed for an instant a jewel – the very jewel which the uncatchable man was even now frantically searching for.

Kate Marshall Flaherty

Magnificat

    I am the lily
in this story.
    On my slender stalk
in an earthen vessel, I'm leaning
my curved white ear
to listen –
In a quiet corner,
Mary is whispering a prayer.
She covers her eyes
with cupped palms. A gentle
breeze from the open window
bends me closer –
I feel a cool breath.
    My petals lift.
The candle on the table wavers;
Mary tips her head back and
takes her hands from her watered eyes.
The soft root of her tongue
silent, still,
she draws in air.
    My own stoma keenly open.
A tear slides down her rose cheek
and yet my roots feel refreshed!
This droplet of water magnifies
everything: her beaming face,
nodding head, and some magnificent
invisible flowering.

Yaqoob Ghaznavi

Red Dress

you showed me the beauty of red
though even now I cannot say
how it made you special
different

I was already in love

maybe I did not know
the meaning of passion

or a proper way of seeing

a field of sunflowers
burning ocean
earth on fire

gold
melting
breathing
dancing

and a yellow flower
pinned to your dress

Len Gasparini

Poinsettia

Outside the window of my room
December snow lights up the darkness.
Tchaikovsky's *First Symphony* is playing
On the clock radio.

In its clay pot a poinsettia glows.
Each whorl of bright red bracts
Surrounds a tiny yellow flower cluster
And fans out into space – to the very edge

Of that space the lower leaves
Fill with green shadows.
From the strain of so much self-illumination
The poinsettia's fragrance is exhausted.

Domenico Capilongo

roses

soft sub-rosa whispers under petals. in the dry palms of lovers. held
wet between lips of tangoed up dancers. the growing of thorns
when cupid shot an arrow in a rose garden by mistake. they bleed
from hot veins. from the red of scarlet letters that spell out sin in
lost latin. your lips perfect velvet roses chapped from winter now
bloom into the fullness of spring kisses. time to dead-head through
forgotten afternoons. *roses are red, roses are red, roses are red ...* sales
were down last year. the florist tells me of women who call her
crying because their roses haven't opened. she tells them to check
the water but really wants them to check their hearts for
unforgiving truths. remember this as your grip on rose hips
tightens. they contain more vitamin c than fruits and vegetables.
cook red roses into a sweet jam and spread it all around the lip of a
trumpet. like miles did before playing into the deep cool jazz-filled
night. the scent of roses melting into the air a sweet smoke. come on
robbie, *my luve's like a red, red rose?* it wilts. it dies. it feeds the
fungus of a globally warmed month of june. roses overflowing with
subsexual sighs soak red into thorns wrapped to make a crown of
new found love. place a petal on the tongues of dead husbands to
sweeten the breath of the hereafter. I can hear her voice before
falling asleep *a rose is a rose is a rose ...*

Wendy Prieto

Snapdragon

Today I am alone.
I cleaned out that small drawer in the basement,
found a blue glove, a trowel, a hook and a length of thin wire.
I found the seeds for those snapdragons and now, I am
tempted to have them grow, to be reminded of their deception:

When I hit her, my tiny daughter would wait for
twilight to whisper to the roses in our garden and
weep into their openness
like one weeps into the face of the beloved,
the cold shock-weight sometimes breaking them,
the flower always the centre of the face always the
moment of deception hooked like new petals hooked
like the child's belief of child and cousin and
childandfatherandchildandfathercousinloverfather.

And I remembered the two of them leaning all
over each other the two doubled over in the
dew-sharp grass, the child much smaller than
her cousin, the child laughing into her
father's fingers pressed all over her blossom.
This is where he teaches her to manipulate the lips;
this is where the snapdragons speak,
(thumb on one side forefinger on the other
push them gently and the flower does open;
this is where the tongue is located: in the heart of a dragon).

Today I am alone.
I will plant the seeds.
I will bury my hand into a blue glove
I will fill my fingers with earth and trowel
I will pierce with the hook and hang off the wire....
And all this is from memory,
oh my shapeless, little, undressed flower!

My garden will heave snapdragons:
not to see them leaning over each other
doubled over in dew-sharp grass, some
smaller, some less innocent than others.
Rather, to watch them die after a season of
growth, the cold, perennial shock-weight
hitting the centre of face, breaking seed and blossom.

Chris Pannell

Six Purple Tulips

blossoms white to curled red
yellow vine threads nodding heads
wasp hovers over
        this green arras and makes
a living weave of last year's ideas
who would believe huge waves in suburban gardens?
        Earth has burst the bulbs
        as you promised, as you planned

my arms ache from the vibrating
hard handle of lawn mower, twisting blunt shears
along the edge
but now the job is done

air brushes my cheek
stripped of stress I can gaze
at the short grass, eye tricked with sweat

suddenly
        six purple tulips
        royal heads
spring
        bright cups of colour
        on straight green stems

make this the moment of your return

Karen Shenfeld

These Infinite Daily Things

Water ripple of
grain across
planed oak;
a gilded frame
reflecting back
the sun's amber;
weight of
the lamp's
hand-wrought iron
stand, its shade,
a bleached bell-
flower; not to forget,
the sofa's cotton
brocade; a diamond-
cut crystal vase,
from which
stalks of willow
lance the air,
each furred bud
nestled still
in its crackled
paper palm;
below them,
an artist's russet
reds and browns,
gold-veined,
slyly marbling the
hearth's drab stone.
These infinite,
daily things –
like the man you
live with,
but no longer see,
until you open
your astonished eyes.

My friend Baila
says, "Divine reality
plays itself out in
the domestic sphere,
and nowhere else."
This morning,
the carpet's
silk flash
as you trod
its bed of
lotus, peony, and rose,
crossing the living-
room, to the kitchen,
where he stood,
backlit, before
the counter, grinding
fragrant beans.

Donna Langevin

Flowers of Fall

I love them because
they are not bankers counting
lost leaves and petals, or hoarding
seeds in their pockets.

They are not preachers
steeped in the sermons
urging last minute repentance.

They are not lawyers
cross-examining clouds,
accusing the wind of a raw deal
and petitioning
the weather gods to defer
the sentence of snow.

Nor are these asters and silva,
geraniums, marigolds, mums –
the colours of whiskey and creme de menthe,
russet and plum wines –
the bartenders of public gardens
bingeing what's left of their time.

Most of all, I love these flowers
that neither "toil nor spin"
because they're not teachers like me
on the eve of retirement,
reviewing what's been passed on.

Bruce Meyer

In the Time of the Dinosaurs There Were No Flowers

The world was void
because love was void.
Beauty was hunger
and hunger endless.

What made the world
turn in its sleep
with fingers spread
a touch in the dark?

A first startled blossom
was no more than chance.
In the time of the dinosaurs
there were no flowers.

But suppose their blood
ran warm as ours,
and from feathered arms
looked up one daybreak

and filled the night
with a death of birdsong –
a chorus that wakes us
when lost is forever;

and a patience of stars
that gathered the light
and raised their voices
to exclaim eternity.

A chrysanthemum opening
to the heart of a bee,
the world made praise
because hope was born:

the first startled blossom
was no more than breath
and breath little more
than the sign of life.

Each sign of life
affirms all creation.
The time of the dinosaurs
left us their love.

Frank Giorno

Yellow Lilies

Friends needling each other
Seated round,
Sharing a meal,
Performing their one act plays,
Recalling stories,
Sharing dialogues, monologues dense
With ironic and erotic twists;
Writers, poets daydreaming,
Prying open minds to dangerous ideas,
Unleashing the latest unsuspecting prank,
Smashing glasses much to the waiter's annoyance
And Peter passing seeds for planting
In tiny plastic bags,
While an overheated woolly dog drips drool
A few feet away on the nearby sidewalk –
All this and more
Under the gaze of yellow lilies,
Soaking in a pitcher of lemon water
Among the coffee, bread and wine,
On a summer patio, on a café table;
Petals open wide to the late evening sky –
Radiating, complex
Tranquil waves
Pistils and stamens
Pollinating
The congregants.

Dorothy Sjöholm

haiku

rainbow painting sky –
windblown trilliums elfin white
spill the april rain

Maureen Scott Harris

Shadowy

It was March. Daffodils stormed and blurred in the train's passing –
along the speckled roadbed, from churchyards, at the foot of every
garden – no dance, but a pour of yellow. My forehead pressed
against the train window, my eyes dazed. O to be *(I was)* in England
now.

The coach rocked, I felt dizzy, closed my eyes, opened them again
and stared at tossing daffodils through my own face reflected in the
glass. Near-transparent, features rising then submerging through
smears of yellow. Self all but erased.

We walked a damp footpath beside a meadow stippled yellow.
Small river catching the light, clumps of sturdy daffodils spilling
down its banks – like a picture in a child's book – yellow cups and
saucers, green spears.

It's March again. Snow smudges my study window and spring's
lost in the middle distance. I stare at the swirling flakes
remembering you and yellow daffodils, pale fluttering inside the
storm.

remembering my mother

Sandra Kasturi

Things the Rose Tree Knows in Spring
for Helen & Dan

The rose tree knows little of love.
It dreams, as all flowering creatures dream,
of things it does know:
wind, the small rain and falling thunderstorm.
The speaking of magpies,
the scurries of round, brown mice.

The rose tree knows even the step
and rattle of postmen,
the hollow bark
of the neighbours' dog
and the shivering
of too-early lilies in their nearby beds.

The rose tree dreams, not of love,
but of openings: one bud, then others,
each a scarlet kiss,
a burst of future –
planting's promise,
the marriage of elements.

The rose tree remembers
and dreams of its storybook counterparts,
thick and thorny and secretive,
growing over paths and princesses;
and of its wild brethren,
small and hardy, hiding
from the hot summer tar
of roads and ways,
and the places roads lead to.

The rose tree dreams of roofs and walls
(so close!) and the two lives ticking inside,
clocks sped up by joy, by joining –
shoes together in the cupboard
or running up the curling staircase,
two pillows, mingled books and songs,
new basil slanting on the window ledge,
artemisia downy-soft in the garden.

The rose tree now remembers
the sun's coming fierceness and the gift
of manmade rain from a pierced tin can,
of hands that peat and mulch and prune together.
Hands that till and turn the earth,
grow roses, trees, turn house to home.

What the rose tree knows and dreams is true.
It now knows love, as loved things do.

Emily Hearn

a sunflower
turns its face
to the sun

has the sun
ever
noticed?

of all my green
and thriving plants
the one that stays
supremely blooming
with tiny scarlet
twinned-flowers
symmetrically
perfect
is that
so bitterly named
for blood
CROWN OF THORNS

Gianna Patriarca

Il Giglio
for Elizabetta

they are tall and elegant
like ladies at a garden party
standing in their finest
warbling on about nothing
sipping the afternoon away
without concern

they are blue-purple velvet
the colour of royal drapes
inside the private towers
of privileged eyes

in her garden they were white
and grew by the gate where
Elizabeth fell on the rocks
a bloodless crevice on
the back of her tender head
she had just learned to walk

her mother wailed by the gate
for years
on her knees
on the same stones
that had absorbed the blood
until the white lamb appeared
by moonlight one night
her mother stopped wailing then
went on weeping in private

i remember the white iris
their lamb's ears
floppy and soft in the
midnight light
they grew there among
the rocks by the gate

David Livingstone Clink

Flowers
a title poem

Flowers
Flowers and death
Flowers and flowering plants: an introduction to the nature
    and work of flowers and the classification of flowering
    plants
Flowers and insects: some birds and a pair of spiders
Flowers can even bloom in schools: selected readings
    in educational psychology
Flowers for Algernon
Flowers for Hitler
Flowers for the living: a book of short stories
Flowers from the ghetto
Flowers from the volcano
Flowers & fury: poems
Flowers in hell: an investigation into women and crime
Flowers in magnetic fields
Flowers in salt: the beginnings of feminist consciousness
    in modern Japan
Flowers in the blood: the story of opium
Flowers in the dustbin: the rise of rock and roll, 1947-1977
Flowers in the empty house
Flowers of fire: twentieth-century Korean stories
Flowers of heaven: one thousand years of Christian verse
Flowers of the night
The flowers of thirst: love poems
Flowers on a one-way street
Flowers on my grave: how an Ojibwa boy's death helped break
    the silence on child abuse
Flowers on stone: a collection of current poems
Flowers on the grass: a novel.

Maureen Hynes

Amaryllis

From my old second floor window
I could watch the writers pick their way
down my leafy street. The disappointed poet
accompanied her nieces home from the school
at the end of my block; the novelist couple
wrangled their large chestnut dog down the sidewalk;
the columnists – there were several – strode
into the coffee shop, sat down and read for hours.
Here, I look for the pianists and the children they teach,
the harpist and all the actors, the photographer who has switched
to acrylics. I have waited for the door to open

in the green house opposite, to glimpse
the strong spirit of the printmaker
whose four months to live
spread to four years. I have watched the amaryllis
in her bay window, the stretching of its stem, its bud
cracking into two fingers, then four: widening, opening,
trumpeting. The plant, a purchase of more time,
has flowered without her.

Luciano Iacobelli

Flower Poem

There's no doubt
that flowers are beautiful
but after smelling them
admiring them for their colour and shape
what can one do with them

I for one
de-petal them

    been doing so
ever since I was a kid
        bloom by bloom
     pulling apart
my family's garden

For a long time I couldn't understand
What I had against these natural artworks
but now
       older
after so many elaborate
       deconstructions
I understand the reason

It's not that I want to rape the flower
   because I'm resentful
       of its inhuman symmetry
It's that I envy the creator's ability
To make things from nothing

By dismantling the rose
I do all a mortal could do
Experience in reverse the self-satisfaction
God must have felt
      after making the world

Jim Christy

Cape Fear

Darling, Sarracenia: I found
you amongst bog and rocky
outcroppings, struck dumb
that such glory flowered
in a meager soil. You stood
alone, no neighbours, neither
rose nor nasturtium for those
were not the bougainvillea
lands. A stranger to your
parts, I learned you succeed
where others perish. Unaware
of your pitfall traps, I would
tumble to all of them.
When you vowed to digest me, I
thought it fancy talk. You
showed the operculum covering your
opening, and I entered like a pilgrim,
a penitent, a prisoner long without,
and reveled in the mucilage. Who
could have resisted when from
your peristope nectar flowed. And
I was trapped. That sweetness
being coniine, same found
in hemlock.
And the way out sealed
by thorns and tendrils.

Steven McCabe

Bouquet Au Lait

Asters without immune systems
Predicting psychic phenomena
Asters without immune systems wrapping themselves
Around your lesser thigh bleeding psychic phenomena
Into your bloodstream

Tulips uninvited draping themselves across your bed
Orange blossoms trailing across the floor around the corner beneath
The door

Wisteria with mouths ejaculating prophecy
Wisteria with bandaged heads limping on crutches celebrating
Victory in the war on soil

Violets with green pages turning like the leaves in a book
Violets accusing in the corner of your dreams
Disappearing as you open your eyes beneath a burning tree
Violets who survive Hiroshima blackened like rusted heaps of
  mangled iron

Baby's breath shedding teardrops
As you adjust your wristwatch baby's breath shedding teardrops

Magnolia pressing voluptuous breasts into you as you drink wine
On the outdoor patio
Daisies wrapping themselves around your TV as you watch 'Law
  and Order'

Black-eyed Susans wearing too much mascara
Trolling the bullfight arena for sweaty customers

Lilacs who mock St. Francis of Assisi
Lilacs showering your naked lover
Lilacs inside your radio

Carnations defusing improvised explosive devices on the side of the
  road
Carnations befriending Mozart in his time of deepest need

Zinnia disbelieving crop circles
Lilies-of-the-valley anticipating Georgia O'Keefe
Lavender smelling of damp soil with a hint of rotting fish
Poppies who love the Rolling Stones

Forget-me-nots shaking their heads at the mention of suicide belts

Dahlias with spikes and horns and sharp ivory teeth crawling
  through the jungle beneath
A full moon
Primrose in a clay pot praying for legalized euthanasia

Sunflowers cheating on you with your wife
Snowdrops with vast white petals obscuring the meteor shower

Orchids perform throat surgery
Orchids spiral around your ankles
Orchids stroke your calves massaging away the sounds
You cannot tune out

The laughter of a newborn iris
The bare shoulders of a pink rose
The Sumerian cremation of a jasmine garland
The buzzing in your ears
The taste of honey on your fingers your eyelids your earlobes
The busy hands collecting pollen-spores from your skin
The sleeplessness as they land, collect and vanish

Sasha Manoli

Suicide Lilies

Your body
underneath so much earth
is a net
full with every flower
imagined and imaginary

*At the last minute
did you want to turn back?*

And to this you reply
with thousands of
white lilies

Growing
endlessly responding
gently spreading
higher
weaving a garden between
this place and an unnamed heaven

Susan Ioannou

Microcosmic

What if
the universe is
a single spangle of light

and whenever a first breath
flares out of darkness
time and space unfold

like a giant bloom by Georgia O'Keeffe,
new life a microscopic
vein in a yellow petal?

Or fragrance spills inside out
a cosmos of sun-and-star pollen
floating across the roof of a chlorophyll cell?

Would it matter
that God could puff up
time like opal balloons,

nanoseconds
bulging to eons
high on a transparent string,

or puncture infinity
into a mirror
flash?

Who are we to explain
that man is the measure,
not mites or nebulae,

that air is the mother element,
not water, not silver,
not fire?

What if
the whole wonder
does not revolve on our eye

but
blinks us awake
only when a root groans

or an asteroid
winds up night's clock,
tail showering pollen into new worlds?

Maria Jacobs

Home's in the Eye

Michaelmas daisies, goldenrod are weeds. No one would think
to plant them – they just grow in this country where they wish,
pleasing the odd transient roving eye. What is more purple,
yellower than they?

Back home where I was born we had them too, the same but different.
Gulden roede we called the goldenrod, meaning the same.
But *herfstasters* were a washed-out lilac, and their name – nothing
to do with saints or angels – just indicated fact: asters of autumn.
The Dutch must love them, drawing them near and hugging them
close to their homes, not a yard without them.

I hated those flowers. Their nearness showed their faults. A day or so
and the gold turned dusty beige, the asters' petals curled and greyed,
then stayed that way all the drab month:
cast-iron plants with mildew-powdered leaves
symbols of summer gone.

But here in Canada, I see the roadsides blaze purpler than purple
and the yellowest yellow. Like its people, this country's flowers:
lovelier because remote.

Corrado Paina

Flowers

at my age one courts
the petals of life
one doesn't pick them any longer
I mean at my age one finally stops
promising castles and diamonds
time's already wasted
at my age one flirts with a flower
flirts with the smell

flowers can be worse than human beings

Andréa Jarmai

Widow's Weeds
Chomolungma Speaks

Here's rosemary.
That's for remembrance
of lost time. And lady's-smock,
for a fair camouflage,
my speckled lord Mallory.
I give you anemone
at the extremity of anger;
that you may see
the whiteness of your body
shine as your dark wounds
glisten here, on Mons Veneris,
and Bertillon's countless
petal-points. Though fearless,
the snowdrop is not the first,
nor the crocus. It is
the mathematics of crystal,
of calyx. Snow is the second
skin. No two alike.

Halli Villegas

Orchid

I once knew a man who kept orchids a secret flower the flower of obsession their petals like skin in variety like sex organs in shape wrinkled pouch of the testicles hanging below the soft white of hidden skin scent heady and opiate a drug to reasonability explorers unused to the tropical heat dazzled by the colours the delicacy of the hidden orchids beneath the canopy of the jungle domesticated they need constant attention special light mistings at appointed hours a lifetime of work for the ephemeral the pale heads would tremble on their stalks when we kissed watchful this too was secret the kiss and the flower.

He offered me the sap of the orchid on the tip of his finger it glistened clear when I took it on my tongue it tasted sweet.

Carla Hartsfield

Afterglow

Flowers with truncated lives:
morning glory, hibiscus, passion flower.
The vine flowers open as I open,
voluptuous convex wet
with night dew, draw

you in, your finger painting
every bulbous vein straining
for wind-caresses, respond,
surprised at the inclination
to express love this quickly.

We try backing up, twirl
patient and oblique
as sun melting slow, so slow,
spills fire at the edge of us,
our bodies not quite awash

but starting to reach toward
strawberry light. I am too susceptible,
yearning, a rose-flush spreading
from crescent to throat, as if
touched by stinging nettle.

I wonder if the vine flowers
ever pray for more breath?
Before a bluing night-canvas
shuts them down, those
wall-eyed stars.

Have they felt my dip and swoon,
bringing images of blood-pooled
stamens pulsing loneliness?
You worry about moving
our emotional clocks forward.

Your fears are not mine.
I know how much I resemble
the tweedy, finicky nature
of the vine flowers, the damage
caused by lack of attention

to all my vulnerabilities.
Then take me away. Do not
show me when spring
leaps out of the snaking
muddy ground. Because

I will keep metamorphosing
into a hybrid, threatening
to stretch the new horizon
our bodies share
into intimate witchery.

Where we, along with the vine flowers,
finally get an answer, more
than expected: permanent
afterglow. Unstaked,
we hide no longer.

Catherine Penny

Fragrant Garden

The abolitionist has been long gone
Rosa Parks did what she had to do
and in Savannah,
the lazy home
to Johnny Mercer,
and take away cocktails,
architecture was the visual reminder
of the stench of that long ago time.
White sidewalks
Black alleyways
Now all lead
To where the blind can see
The sun
The rain
The yellow white of jasmine
The gentle pink of magnolia
The honeysuckle and gardenia
Hummingbirds and milkweed
Its vanilla
interspersed with
Angel Face and Buff Beauty
Hiding spots for wrens and robins
with thorns to puncture
the bleeding hearts
The fragrant garden
Can
Lead
To where the blind can see

Lynda Curnoe

Mourning the Future of a Bunch of Orange Tulips

Who makes coffee with Melitta filters anymore?
Pouring boiling water into a plastic paper-lined cone –
just a little bit at first to wet the coffee – then more
until the cup line is reached.
Watching the liquid drip into a thin glass carafe
Takes forever.
Unscientific
and weak.

When he handed me the tulips I said
There isn't a vase here.
Why not put them in the coffee pot?
They fit so neatly like they were home –
and from tight buds
now elegantly opening up full
as though singing
with more and more passion.

But if I leave tomorrow
they will continue opening up
without me seeing them
until they sing so loud
their petals fall off.

And when I come back
yellowed stems will be
sticking out of the coffee pot
shrivelled orange bits
displayed on the table and floor.

I don't want to come back to see that.
But can't throw them away
now
just as they are.

Isabella Colalillo Katz

Spring unfolding on the streets of Toronto

first the snowdrops
naked among snowfields and the patchy northern wind
that lacerates my skin
crocus next: yellow and purple in thick crowds
among them the rain and daffodils,
playful in white & yellow caps deep in meditation
as if dreaming birds into being;
they listen as I walk by,
mute and beautiful.
here and there some bold-faced tulips
among hyacinths clutching purple and pink
in grapelike clumps as if afraid to be alone.
the iris and lilies wait.
pussy willows shout above the rooftops.
cherry blossoms puff and gather in my garden
among the forsythia
opening tiny gambage mouths to yellow sunlight
against warm walls or air
& today among the Monet blue scylla
gathering around the maple
she was a blazing queen
watching their blue eyes open to grassgreen songs
already fading as the rain comes
& the earth's womb opens envelopes of light
membranes of loveliness
fresh promises
Eden is reborn
reborn as magnolia blossoms floating in pink gowns;
they dance and signal
like a thousand Cinderellas decked out for the ball
then as I wander down Belgravia
there in front of the bakery,
a pink cherry, a *sakura*, in her Asian accent
speaks to me of my childhood house on Crawford Street
her sister flowering on the lawn those many years now gone

it seems a reverie, not real
but her blossoms gather in my heart just the same,
as if they were Ulysses and his stories
come home again to Ithaca.

Kenneth Sherman

Bee Balm

Their petals are a deep red
Set off against green leaves
And the white astilbes
Planted next to them in your painter's garden.

You said they were curative –
A remedy for heart disease,
A prescription
To work against dejection.

The ancients would say they grew
From a lover's wound,
Or drifted up from the underworld –
Spirits vivid but speechless.

Strange to think such colour
Rose out of darkness,
Nourished by nothing more
Than see-through water and light.

Now that their tufts
Have shriveled and fallen
All that remains is that alliteration
I first heard on your lips.

Ray Ellenwood

A Pair of Wild Flowers

1. *Jack-in-the-pulpit*

Look for me
Damp in calvinist shade
Green among green
Disguised.
Of my conical pulpit,
Lift the shy flap,
See my deep purple
Staff.

2. *Black-eyed susan*

Not your prim, white, eastern
Daisy's
My brown tuft
And buckskin petals.

Ludwig Zeller

Carnation Stems

An old woman follows me offering a few carnations
I tell her no, that where would I put them?
She holds out her hand and looks into my eyes,
Twenty pesos, she says, and beautiful – perhaps, sir,
You might want them, might need them...
                                        I give in and the first
Acquaintance I meet, I tell her they flowered for her.

I am not sure why I had to write these poems,
These flowers in letters, calligraphy, here in the last
Days of my life that follow me and light little lights
To say both love and friendship exist – Imagine!
Here they are – you might perhaps want them,
                    or like me, perhaps need them.

English translation by Joan Lindgren

Karl Jirgens

Dream Flowers

       In a dream the night before,
outside, gazing at earth, garden, leaves
of grass, rocks, and small wildflowers in a meadow,
my hand opened to touch one of the blooms
to find large rubies rooted in my palms.
I wondered at this, and touched the palm
of each hand. The ruby ice.
Palms swaying in the breeze.

Sitting, without reason my hands rose
to my eyes and I wept. After a time, tears
subsided. With a wipe a world transformed.
Everything, as far as the eye could see
was red. Not uniform, but instead,
myriad reds, warm and cool, with
different readings of temperature.
Reading the hues, intense, or faint,
alizarin crimsons, teeming scarlets,
impassioned pinks, seductive burgundies,
all seemed lush and terrifying. And when
I looked to my hands, the rubies
were gone.

I thought, "An eye of stone, can still see
with peerless clarity. An eye of grenadine, at twilight
sights the royal purples, while night brings
the violet's serene violence, until morning
a splash of crimson sun, and day, the tinted glass of air
flows over with syllables unuttered, and broken speech,
a failure of metaphor is read, elliptic, a semi-conductor,
or element, not an empty clearness, nor bottomless sight,
not an empty glass, instead, a visible trace of thought, or speech
  unspoken.
The fire-eye of the sun rotates above, through the dance of trope,
through spectrums of the purple heart, the shape and size of things,

a measure of them as they are, an unspoken apostrophe, a red
 thought
read, and beyond recall."
All this I remembered as I awoke to a world of colour.

To relate such a dream, I thought, is not difficult, nor uncommon.
But suppose, I thought, we lived in a world of red, for all our days,
and grew adjusted as we did when watching silent movies,
or later, the cinema or television of black and white.
Suppose there was nothing more, but shades and hues of a single
 colour,
a gray scale of a sort, but in red alone, from dark to light, and then,
 one day
perhaps someone dreamed   of a world of colour, beyond the
 monochrome,
what words could there be to relate such a thing ...

Dennison Smith

Moonflower

At noon can I hear the grass breathe,
The apple blossom moan?

No not at noon.
So the poem is the voice of twilight.

Before the chalk earth cracks in the rape fields,
Before the alabaster summers rush into arroyos,

When the rope becomes the snake
And all is changeful,

In twilight's white, the Moon-flower,
Chalice of the mouthy Eve-churr

Who in legend sucks the milk from goats,
Hunts the baffled moths,

White like the bones of water,
Salt flats of once oceans,

Lost snow,

Twilit-plucked and dead by morning,

Its loud perfumed performance
A transitory word.

Lara Solnicki

Flower Shop Keeper

The flower shop keeper is watering
paper white lilies, that fold like origami birds
and African violets, leaking primary colours
from their baby orifices.

He primes the lipstick-red tulips,
heaving like cutlet through their waxy silks,
and purple orchids, fallen aliens
he's dragged up and hung on invisible strings.

He dotes on their severed heads –
mouths open, listless tongues
peeling back at the passersby;
sallow, shriveling circus tents;

As the hanging plants dangle their stars –
helixes unravel inseminating dust,
stars and more stars
glittering and nudging each other,
clusters of infant hands tearing
at each other's tinsel, falling –
yellow squelches echoing in tin pails.

He kneels with his spade, stabs, rousing the pot-soil.
Leaves fall to his ankles,
clumps of slime slide in the guts of grates;
veins jolting like wire
as he feverishly picks up
the dropped petals, the red shreds.

Keith Garebian

Orchids

Emerald veining stone walls
dependent on the generosity of green
as leaves close in,
there's a stir of orchids in partial shade,
an immaculate quivering on stalks
near virgin buds awaiting their turn.
Pigmenting their needs in yellow and white,
chaste tendrils dependably pure though beckoning,
they leave no stain in their unraveling.
The rains have stopped, sunlight
penetrates all green canopies,
but the orchids, intact
on their branches, are pale,
ecstatically soft, and safe.

(Singapore, Apr. 9-10/07)

Mary Lou Soutar-Hynes

what is it
about flowers

that petals us

open   season after season

first a single

bract   then one lone leaf

then trillium—

like to   bud and bloom in

            vestiges of snow

Spring's ephemera —

brief as   anemone's passing breeze

fresh-leaved

shadows   trace the

            veins of

trees —   crown the lawn

soil's seduction

squares of

black earth   sprouting green

from the pond   our wintry

apprehensions —   surface lotus-red

Flavio Belli

The Oceanic Charles Hoarfrost Backstop Rose

About life I missed shouting carefully

A work in progress

Charles Chevy Flower, a heterogeneous depositor of blossoms, read Blake out loud and got the attention of the debaucherous flagstone Figaro Fluctibus, a crystallite catalogue puppy. His reddish brown dome vacuous cloudburst ambling toward a Christmas summertime refectory full of contraband caused a glorious melee that broke out in the sunshine.

Charles' copious inshore factual tumbled pebbles sent a rankled craven courier propelling like a celandine holdout carbonate cloud burst through a wary December bribe. But it was his impolitic backtrack that bent the lame emendable steel.

Using an arteriolosclerosis trombone Charles contrasted a Cumberland Rose with the defendant's aerobic backstop Edmund's Speak and a stray Burgundian Beauty.

His metabolite downtrend attracted Diana who patrolled lantern Nibelungen along dint footpath intended and begetting. How down the page, second year after year told again as a bed time story, his romance of her with flowers lasted a century.

Charles' boyhood disciplinary, even if in particulate, bereaved the Christmas dole and airmail package of posies soon made something almost give. The boys on sentence were asked how long they'd been at times still. It was never but when they bent to the bloom and sniffed.

We've been in the dark quite a while and you may as well explain what happened next.

Why, he created the Oceanic Charles Hoarfrost Backstop Rose!

No more thanks to the severely chamber-faced cute girl who dropped the blue bud vase and ran for preference control, than for all his little round hairy pencils and green odd shaped sport shoes. The soft green carpet stood still while his brother's red door staggered and a given yellow book calmed the children's bluish smiles. And perhaps any silver camera sleeps.

Play before earth hears a night find. Near only five petals, very close and very big, what light comes few understand. The more earth off gives air without sacrificing some of the sweet perfume, the more Philip's barefaced rally street bray tootles the Athenian tortoiseshell, blessedly hale, attentive, cranky and justifiably convulsive.

Charles Chevy Flower and his wife took Turkish Archibald a megawatt Yellow Bullfinch to prove their love. To the Pope they sent an electroencephalogram banker and the Edmund's Speak Rose. There was a determinate sell-out to assemblage Vaticano with stealth and curiosity that eventually allowed the family to calibrate advice and establish the now famous annual Vladivostok concert.

Ch 1, pg 89

Heather Cadsby

Nasturtium Models

They put up sunshades
flat green barriers
to probing eyes and a nasty mood.
Ruffled, layered and
bright enough to burn
they are fed up with shining,
and swaying their skirts.

Do not pull back the plain green veils.
They must catch their breath. Dazzling beauty
needs a dull costume now and then.
Just hold it right there. They may not be bridal.
Stay still awhile.

Later we can know.
I will come to you
fiery, reticent.

Elana Wolff

Astral

Fish, when you return, you may be fern;
Black-eyed Susan: girl. View the human

hinted in the headdress of the rose,
calyx-near to soul.

Celebrate the template,
praise the Maker: What a world –

from structured Love, to dust.
Falling thought, away in light,

forever strewing beauty. Death,
the future here-before, caldera

of adjustment. Malca, my romantic
friend, unlimited now by physics,

I liken you to crocus, gold;
sense your griffin-spirit pulsing in pigment.

Liz Zetlin

Lady's Slipper

Most seem unanimous
in their choice of metaphor.
The Germans say *woman's shoe,*
in Russian, *Mary's slipper.*
Venus' shoe or *shoe of the virgin* in French.
In Ojibwa, *dancing slipper,*
and to Bruce/Grey settlers,
moccasin flower or *squirrel shoe.*
     Even the Greek means
     Aphrodite's little shoe
       and I wonder,
why insist on women's feet
when the swollen flower looks
more like a purse
     or a pout.

The Greeks used to put phallic objects in women's shoes.
     I imagine slender river stones
     bay leaves
     sprigs of oregano.
The Chinese found tiny shoes erotic.
     I see a woman's foot bent
     back on itself
     toes to heel
and then I remember the shoes dangling
under the "just married" sign
     and the nursery rhyme I used to chant
     about the old woman
     who lived in a shoe.

I can feel my mother's arm tighten
around me as she reads the story
of a prince's quest for a foot
to fit his perfect glass slipper.
     I know many women
     who tried to wear that shoe.

Only the Ojibwa and the early settlers
seemed to have a meaning
I want to believe in –
      the importance of dancing
      the comfort of squirrels.

Fraser Sutherland

Allons voir si la rose
– Ronsard

And does the rose
bloom in its accustomed place,
the green at the heart of the rose?

The lilac is full of summer.
Blue, you think of sky,
its pages opened by swallows.

The ripe apple leaps from the bough.
Its seeds taste of almond.
Ash Wednesday, chill water in clay.

New oats and new barley, green, greener,
the wind, hands in their hair
their secret sonata, like fear

the deer have come to the orchard,
cropping at apples. They sweetly crouch
on frozen ground.

The colt and the yearling plunge
in the first moist wind,
kick high into summer.

Go see if the trillium
blooms in the snow. Frost flowers
White. White. White.

The wild rose and the white rose
within their hearts
discovered green.

Christine Thorpe

Do you remember pansies

with their early-rising, foolish grins
clowning under floppy brims?
They seldom reached profusion,
but their faces radiated bonhomie
in pretty, pleasing colours,
and to see them made you smile.

Unsung by poets and,
unlike lavender and lilacs, unscented;
upstaged by peonies and,
unlike the precious roses, untended;
threatened by invasive ivy and
bullied by petunias, they died bravely,
annually, at frost's booted feet.

Then came the "icicle" pansies,
transgenic wonders of the nursery world,
supplanting borders of salvia
and trampling the nasturtiums,
wrestling the ground-cover for a yard
and sending creeping charlie
to cower under the porch.

Icicle pansies don't freeze,
but cuddle under blankets of snow
and spring into March fully-dressed.
Fabulous, firm and faceless,
engendering beauty, yes,
but seldom a smile.

David Reibetanz

vermillion

is not
your colour
aechmea fasciata

what you show the world is
not passion
but
blue
blossomed
from your funnel

marbled green leaves open
bare a heart
dark in root
not pulsing rubens but
reaching up in arcs of bracts

the colour of a blush
so unblooded
so
sheer

that desire must now
stand behind
the touch that
follows

and because they see you
as a child
and do not imagine that even
the way you drink is
wise

you force your blush
into blue bloom
dancing
on the tips
of your rosette

birth of the divine
sapphires
the eyes

while each leaf sprouts
a point
to tell the one who touches
before he looks
otherwise

Phoebe Tsang

Blood Roses

Numbed by the slap of wet concrete when I slipped and fell
to ground, a wreath of blood-roses tattooed my arm:
four blue rosettes with rosebud hearts.

Rain bled through cloth and broken skin to bind body
with the earth beneath. I lay willing to be blessed
or sacrificed. Then I laughed and walked.

They say shock will perform miracles, make you believe
you can close your own wounds, reclaim
the body you had – this is the dangerous part.

To the passers-by who stare from arm's length
and ask if I'm ok, I say: Come take a closer look,
don't be afraid; they're only decorations.

But remember, the body was built as a lair; who knows
what has come in with the rain, the roses and the roots
of roses, with their thorns and rosaries? I rose

as if suddenly awakened, my skin sealed smooth
by rain's witch-doctor fingers, green fingers reclaiming
this elemental body fallen out of my hands, later to bloom
          red and blue and yellow roses.

Priscila Uppal

An Apology

A sincere apology to all the plants I've failed:
the ones that wasted away in corners like spinster aunts
in attics, the ones that crunched into themselves
like imploding stars, or those whose dry leaves fell one
by one, like the slowest arsenic drip.

Indoor, outdoor, I have all kinds of green blood on my hands.
The nights storms rained disaster and I didn't bother
to bring you inside, too worried about soaking my hair,
catching cold, or the buds that never opened because
I was too busy to learn the right spell, kneel down
in the dirt and accept your warbling words, the weeks
I'd be sunning myself in South America or
sipping Cosmopolitans in European cafés, and I told
the housesitter, 'try to remember
to water every day, but if you can't just make sure
the garbage is taken out on time.'
(I should have added an extra hundred
to make sure you were all properly provided for.)

And those of you who sported signs
announcing 'very little water needed'
tricked me into believing we were fast friends, but
I should have known better. I didn't just fall off
the turnip truck like you. And those who were
gifts for great occasions – birthdays, anniversaries,
promotions, even sympathies – for forgetting
about you in your glass houses, I owe you
all individual, dramatic apologies.

But please, allow me to explain why
I let the cats drink out of your reservoirs, snipe
and bite at your fragile limbs:
They never meant to hurt you.
Living things must test out other living things.

Like me, they just floundered in the acts
of demonstrating kindness and consolation.
Unlike you, for whom this is your nature, we go
on neglecting and needing, loving but killing,
not really ever taking the time to say:
'thank you,' or 'miss you,' 'so long,' or 'sorry.'

About the Poets

Flavio Belli is an artist and art consultant. He is also a member of the Board of Directors of the Toronto Outdoor Art Exhibition, the Canadian Cultural Property Export Review Board and the McMurtry Gardens of Justice selection committee.

Steven Michael Berzensky (Mick Burrs) has over 750 poems published so far. *Pages Torn From Trees,* his latest poetry collection, was launched by Lyricalmyrical in 2007. Mick is also a playwright, essayist, editor, & artist. Sings, too.

Ronna Bloom is the author of three books of poetry, most recently, *Public Works* (Pedlar Press, 2004). Her poems have been translated into Spanish and Bangla. She lives in Toronto, where she works as a writer, teacher and psychotherapist. "The Good Plant" was published in *Contemporary Verse 2,* Volume 19 No.4, Spring 1997.

Heather Cadsby is the author of three books of poetry. *A Tantrum of Synonyms* (Wolsak and Wynn) was a finalist for the Pat Lowther Award. In 2006/2007 her poems appeared in *The Antigonish Review, Grain, The Fiddlehead, Dalhousie Review, The Malahat Review,* and *Prism International.*

Domenico Capilongo is published recently in *Filling Station* and *Lichen.* His first book of poetry, *I thought elvis was italian,* is forthcoming with Wolsak and Wynn. He and his family live in Toronto, where you can spot him dead heading roses.

Jim Christy is a writer and visual artist based in Toronto. His latest CD of songs, poems and music, *God's Little Angle,* is released Fall, 2007 by She's Right Records.

David Livingstone Clink is the Artistic Director of the Rowers Pub Reading Series and is the webmaster of poetrymachine.com. He's had poems in *The Antigonish Review, The Fiddlehead, Grain Magazine,* and *The LRC.* His first book of poetry is forthcoming from Tightrope Books, Spring 2008.

Lynda Curnoe's *A Trip Around Grenadier Pond,* a long poem detailing a "trip" around a pond in Toronto's High Park, was published by Lyricalmyrical Press in 2007.

Gary Michael Dault is a Toronto-based writer, artist and poet. His most recent books are *The Milk of Birds* (Mansfield Press, 2006) and *Southwester* (Lyricalmyrical, 2007). Coach House Books is currently producing a limited edition of his *Hebdomeros Suite.* Recent solo exhibitions have included *An Hour of Landscape Painting: Sixty One-Minute Paintings on Cereal Boxes* at Gallery Pagte & Strange in Halifax, and *The Fifty-Minute Hour: Fifty One-Minute Landscapes on Cereal Boxes* at the Michael Gibson Gallery in London, Ontario. His art-review column, "Gallery-Going," appears every Saturday in *The Globe & Mail.*

Kildare Dobbs's autobiography, *Running the Rapids,* is published in Canada by Dundurn Books (Toronto, 2006). In 2000 he was invested with the Order of Ontario.

Paul Dutton is a poet, novelist, essayist, musician, and oral sound artist. He has read and performed, solo and ensemble (the Four Horsemen, CCMC), throughout Europe and North America. Most recent works: *Several Women Dancing* (novel) and *Oralizations* (CD). "Bluebell" has appeared in *The Additives* (Toronto: Imprimerie Dromadaire, 1988) and *Partial Additives* (London, England: Writers Forum, 1994).

Ray Ellenwood has done a number of translations of writers from Québec, including Marie-Claire Blais, Claude Gauvreau, Gilles Hénault, and Jacques Ferron. His most recent publication is a chapbook of translations of poems by Thérèse Renaud entitled *The Sands of Dream* (Toronto: Bookthug, 2007).

Kate Marshall Flaherty's first book, *Tilted Equilibrium,* was published by Hidden Brook Press. She won the Canadian Church Press Best Poem, was shortlisted for *Descant's* Winston Collins Best Canadian Poem and Nimrod's Pablo Neruda Poetry Prize, and was published in *Word, THIS Magazine, Freefall, Other Voices,* and several anthologies.

Keith Garebian of Mississauga was long-listed for the ReLit Award for *Frida: Paint Me As a Volcano* (BuschekBooks, 2004). He has been runner-up in the Dan Sullivan Poetry contest and winner of awards from the Scarborough and Lakeshore Arts Councils.

Gale Zoë Garnett is the author of the novels *Visible Amazement, Transient Dancing,* and *Room Tone,* of which *The Globe and Mail* says "Do not hesitate to purchase this wonderfully realised, beautiful book ...Garnett is a masterly writer. There are elements here of Milan Kundera and Gabriel García Márquez."

Len Gasparini is the author of *The Broken World: Poems 1967-1998.* He has also published three story collections: *Blind Spot, A Demon in My View,* and *The Undertaker's Wife.* "Poinsettia" originally appeared, in a slightly different version, in *Ink from an Octopus* (Hounslow Press, 1989).

In his sixties **Yaqoob Ghaznavi** got bitten by the twin passions of writing poetry and running long-distance. Often he is crazy with one of these obsessions. He has poems published or forthcoming in *Big Pond Rumours, Street #6, Tower Poetry,* and *Carousel.*

Frank Giorno lives in Toronto and is the author of one collection of poetry, *Elvis in America,* published by Lyricalmyrical Press (2006).

Maureen Scott Harris has published *A Possible Landscape* (Brick Books, 1993), *Drowning Lessons* (Pedlar Press, 2004, winner of the Trillium Book Award for Poetry), and the chapbooks *The World Speaks* (Junction Books, 2003) and *The Raven and the Writing Desk* (JackPine Press, 2007).

Carla Hartsfield has had three collections of poetry published. Her most recent, *Your Last Day on Earth* (Brick Books, 2003), was long-listed for the ReLit Award. Carla's poems have appeared in numerous anthologies and journals in Canada and the U.S., and can be found in current issues of *Prairie Fire, Rampike, From the Web,* and *Only the Sea Keeps: Poems of the Tsunami.* Carla is also a singer-songwriter, pianist, koto and autoharp player.

Emily Hearn is well known as a children's song and scriptwriter for CBC radio and TVO, an author of children's books, writer of the Mighty Mites natural history strip for *OWL* magazine, editor of children's readers for Nelson Canada, and poet of adult books *Grass of Green Moment* (Pendas) and *They Look Like This to Me* (Hidden Brook Press), in which these two poems appeared in 2006.

Maureen Hynes, a past winner of the Gerald Lampert Prize and a recent winner of Britain's Petra Kenney Prize, is working on her third poetry manuscript, *The Geometry We Want.* She teaches at George Brown College in Toronto.

Luciano Iacobelli is the editor and publisher of Lyricalmyrical Press and a partner in Quattro Books. He is the author of numerous chapbooks and one full-length book of poetry entitled *The Angel Notebook,* published by Seraphim Editions in the Spring of 2007.

Susan Ioannou is a Toronto editor whose poetry, fiction, and literary articles have appeared across Canada. Her most recent collections are *Coming Home: An Old Love Story* (Leaf Press) and *Looking Through Stone: Poems about the Earth* (Your Scrivener Press). "Microcosmic" appeared in *Where the Light Waits* (Ekstasis Editions, 1996).

Maria Jacobs has several books of poetry, and one autobiography, *A Safe House.* She has collected, edited, and translated poetry from the Dutch, *With otherwords.* For the past 25 years, she has owned Wolsak and Wynn Publishers and though now retired from the business, she still edits the poetry collections for the press.

Andréa Jarmai's first major collection of poetry, *Brother to Dragons, Companion to Owls,* was published by Seraphim Editions in 2004. Her translation of George Faludy's "Michelangelo's Last Prayer" appears on a bronze plaque in *George Faludy Place* in Toronto.

Karl Jirgens, Head of English (University of Windsor), is Editor-in-chief of *Rampike,* a critically acclaimed international journal of art and literature, and author of numerous internationally published articles, as well as four books (with Coach House, ECW, and Mercury Presses).

Sandra Kasturi's first full-length poetry collection, *The Animal Bridegroom,* came out in June, 2007 from Tightrope Books. She is currently working on a collection of sonnets as well as an animated children's TV series. In 2005 she won *ARC* magazine's annual Poem of the Year award for her poem "Old Men, Smoking." Sandra's poetry has also appeared in various magazines and anthologies, including several of the *Tesseracts* series. She is a founding member of the Algonquin Square Table poetry workshop, and runs her own imprint, Kelp Queen Press.

Isabella Colalillo Katz is a writer/poet, storyteller, educator, editor and psychotherapist. She has published two books of poetry, *Tasting Fire* (1999) and *And Light Remains* (2006), both from Guernica Editions. She leads workshops and classes on personal creativity and writing, and has presented her creative and scholarly work at many international conferences. Her poetry and prose has appeared in magazines, journals, and anthologies. She has given numerous storytelling and poetry performances in Canada and internationally and been featured on CBC radio.

Donna Langevin's poems have been published in numerous journals in Canada and the USA. Her books of poetry include *Improvising in the Dark* (watershedBooks, 2000) and *The Second Language of Birds* (Hidden Brook Press, 2005).

Sasha Manoli is a Creative Writing Student at Concordia University. In February 2006 her chapbook *To My Veins* was published by Lyricalmyrical Press. She is also the co-creator of WithWords Press, a small discovery chapbook press located in Montreal.

Steven McCabe is a Toronto poet and visual artist. He is the author of four books of poetry, most recently *Hierarchy of Loss* (Ekstasis Editions, 2007).

Lynn McClory is grateful to the magazines *BafterC, Psychic Rotunda, Industrial Sabotage,* and *Poetry Mag* on blissfultimes.ca for publishing her poems. Appreciation also to Les Mardistes, Lexiconjury, for a chapbook *10 Poems,* written during Phil Hall's workshop, and to Stuart Ross for encouragement and poems written at his poetry boot camps.

Bruce Meyer is author of 26 books, including 7 collections of poetry as well as *The Golden Thread* and *Heroes.* He teaches for Laurentian University at Georgian College.

Corrado Paina has published *Hoarse Legend, The Dowry of Education,* and *the alphabet of the traveller* with Mansfield Press and has also published a number of books in Italy. He is the editor with Denis De Klerk of the book *College Street/Little Italy – The Renaissance Strip,* recently published by Mansfield.

Chris Pannell has published two poetry books: *Under Old Stars* and *Sorry I Spent Your Poem*. He serves on the organizing committee for the Hamilton reading series Lit Live and on the board of the annual GritLiT literary festival. His most recent poetry manuscript is entitled *Driven*. "Six Purple Tulips" was previously published in *Sorry I Spent Your Poem* (watershedBooks).

Gianna Patriarca has published 6 books of poetry and one children's book. Her writing is extensively anthologized and her work has been adapted for the stage and radio. "Il Giglio" is from *My Etruscan Face* (Quattro Books).

Jaclyn Piudik earned an MA in Poetry from the City College of New York. Her poems have been published in *WV Magazine, Poetry in Performance Anthology, Columbia Poetry Review, Sojourner, Crosscurrents*, and *Barrow Street*. She is the author of a chapbook, *The Tao of Loathliness*, published by fooliar press in 2005. Jaclyn is the recipient of a New York Times Fellowship for Creative Writing, the Goodman Fund Grant for Excellence in Creative Writing, and the Sellers Award from the Academy of American Poets.

Catherine Penny, a native of Nova Scotia, grew up with four brothers across Canada and overseas. Earns a living as a business person. She has poems in the anthology *Renaissance Reloaded* (Aeolus House, 2006).

Robert Priest is the author of fifteen books of poetry, 3 plays, 2 novels, lots of musical CDS, one hit song, and many columns for *Now Magazine*. His words have been debated in the legislature, posted in the Transit system, quoted in the *Farmer's Almanac,* and sung on *Sesame Street.* AKA Dr. Poetry. For more see: youtube.com/greatbigfaced or poempainter.com. A new book, *Backwards*, will be published by ECW in 2008.

Wendy Prieto is a Canadian writer of Hispanic background, currently a student at Glendon, York University. In May 2006 some of her work was published as a chapbook by Lyricalmyrical Press, entitled *No Amount of Weeping.*

David Reibetanz has published poetry in journals and collections such as *echolocation, The Fiddlehead, In Fine Form,* and *Poetry as Liturgy.* He has won The Hart House Poetry Prize, the Pratt Poetry Medal, and the Petra Kenney Poetry Prize (Young Poets). His chapbook, *Blue Fire,* was published with Junction Books.

Rob Rolfe is the author of two chapbooks, *The Crooked Bridge* (Lyricalmyrical, 2005) and *The Tracks of the Dead* (Lyricalmyrical, 2007). His poems have also appeared in *The Fiddlehead, Grain, The Prairie Journal, This Magazine, Impulse,* and *Our Times.*

Karen Shenfeld is a Toronto poet, writer, and filmmaker. She has published two books of poetry with Guernica Editions: *The Law of Return* (1999), which won a Canadian Jewish Book Award, and *The Fertile Crescent* (2005). Her poetry has appeared in numerous Canadian and international journals.

Kenneth Sherman has published several collections of poetry. His most recent is *Black River* (Porcupine's Quill, 2007). His collection of essays, *A Violence from Within,* is forthcoming. "Bee Balm" was published in *The Well: New and Selected Poems* (Wolsak and Wynn, 2000).

Sue Sinclair's latest collection of poems, *Days Without End,* will be published by Brick Books in 2008. Her previous collections have been nominated for various national awards. Sue is currently studying philosophy at the University of Toronto. "Roses" appeared in her collection *Mortal Arguments* (Brick Books, 2003), and before that, in *The Malahat Review* (Winter 2001).

Dorothy Sjöholm's poems have appeared in Canadian and British journals and anthologies including *Aesthetica, Lichen, Jones Av, Renaissance Reloaded,* and *Myth Weavers,* and have received recognition from the Scarborough Arts Council, Lichen, The Writers' Circle of Durham Region, and The Ontario Poetry Society.

Poet, novelist and playwright, **Dennison Smith** has published in most mediums in the U.S., Canada and England. Her novel, *Scavenger,* was published with Insomniac Press. The poetry collection, *Anon Necessity,* is forthcoming from Lyricalmyrical. She's presently working on her new novel.

Lara Solnicki is a writer of poetry and experimental prose, a classical singer, a contemporary music collaborator, and private music teacher. "Flower Shop Keeper" appeared in her first book of poems, *Disassembled Stars* (Lyricalmyrical Press, 2006). Lara is currently working on a second Lyricalmyrical book, to be released in 2008.

Mary Lou Soutar-Hynes is a Jamaican-Canadian poet/educator. Recent publications: her second collection, *Travelling Light* (Seraphim Editions, 2006), long-listed for the 2007 ReLit Poetry Award, and work in *Calling Cards: New Poetry from Caribbean/Canadian Women* (Sandberry Press, 2005).

Fraser Sutherland is a writer and editor who lives in Toronto. His most recent poetry collection is *Manual for Emigrants* (Tightrope Books). "Allons voir si la rose" was published in *Nebula 13* (ca. 1979-80) and reprinted subsequently.

Christine Thorpe is a native of Penticton, B.C., a graduate of the University of Toronto and Carleton University, and a resident of London, Ontario. She is currently preparing a manuscript of poems, many of which were written during a recent stay in Wellington, New Zealand (where camellias bloom in the winter).

Phoebe Tsang was born in Hong Kong, grew up in England, and has been resident in Canada since 1998. She has published two chapbooks, *Solitaires* (2006, Lyricalmyrical Press) and *To Kiss the Ground* (2007, Press On!). Her poetry is published in journals worldwide, including *Atlas 02* (India). A professional violinist, she also holds a BSc in Architecture. www.phoebetsang.com.

Priscila Uppal's book publications include: *How to Draw Blood From a Stone* (1998); *Confessions of a Fertility Expert* (1999); *Pretending to Die* (2001); *The Divine Economy of Salvation* (2002); *Live Coverage* (2003); and *Ontological Necessities* (2006), a Griffin Poetry Prize finalist.

Halli Villegas has written two books of poetry, *Red Promises* (Guernica Editions, 2001) and *In the Silence Absence Makes* (Guernica Editions, 2004), and a chapbook, *The Human Cannonball* (Believe Your Own Press, 2005). She is the owner and publisher of Tightrope Books.

Ewan Whyte has written for *The Globe and Mail* and *Books in Canada*. His short stories, translations and reviews have been published in literary journals and magazines and he has read his translations of Catullus on Public Radio in the U.S. His translation of the poetry of Catullus was published in 2004. He is currently finishing a novel and translating the complete poetry of Horace.

Elana Wolff's most recent book of poetry is *You Speak to Me in Trees* (Guernica, 2006), a portion of which was short-listed for the 2004 CBC Literary Award for Poetry. She is currently working on a collection of short essays on poems of GTA poets.

Ludwig Zeller is the author of some 50 books of poetry, collages and fiction. Born in Chile, Zeller made Toronto his home for 24 years before moving to Oaxaca, Mexico. Latin American critic J.M. Oviedo has referred to Zeller as "the last of the Surrealists." *The Eye on Fire* (Ekstasis, 2007) is the latest of his poetry collections to appear in English translation.

Paul Zemokhol lives and writes in Toronto. His first chapbook, *Apocrypha*, was published in 2005. His second chapbook, *No Hope, No Help, No Tea*, will be launched in 2007.

Liz Zetlin is a poet (*The Thing With Feathers*) and filmmaker (*Limestone Ghazals, Pond, Nightwalk*). She is currently Owen Sound's first Poet Laureate, co-artistic director of the Words Aloud Spoken Word Festival, and co-producer/director of this year's Festival Documentary. "Lady's Slipper" is from *Taking Root* (Seraphim Editions, 2001).